THE GOLDEN COMPASS™

IOREK

and the

Gyptian Alliance

NEW LINE CINEMA
A Time Warner Company

SCHOLASTIC INC.
New York Toronto London Auckland Sydney
Mexico City New Delhi Hong Kong Buenos Aires

ISBN-13: 978-0-545-05932-9
ISBN-10: 0-545-05932-1

12 11 10 9 8 7 6 5 4 3 2 1   8 9 10 11 12 13/0

Printed in the U.S.A.   01

This printing, February 2008

CHAPTER ONE

*T*he mighty bear sank his razor-sharp teeth into the leg of reindeer meat.

He hadn't eaten all day and he was hungry. *Very* hungry. So hungry that he was even prepared to scavenge amongst rubbish for food like a common thief, instead of hunting for prey like the great Panserbjørne he had once been.

In the bitterly cold Northern port of Trollesund, everyone knew of the Panserbjørne – a fearsome group of armoured Ice Bears. Loyal, clever and very strong, they were formidable warriors, respected by all and feared by many. Most were employed by the Magisterium – the organization that told everyone what to do.

But not this bear.

Iorek Byrnison was different. He was an outcast, earning barely enough to survive. Even worse, he had no armour. And an armoured bear without armour is just a bear.

The shadows stretched longer and longer as the sun sank towards the horizon. It became colder, the frozen mud beneath Iorek's feet turning as hard as iron. Hardly aware of the noise from the nearby bar or the approach of night, the huge creature sank his teeth again into the hunk of meat. It was hardly the tastiest meal he'd ever had, but he gnawed hungrily all the same.

Suddenly, there were footsteps, but Iorek ignored them. No one ever came to see him. He was a nobody.

'Iorek Byrnison!' The man's voice was deep, powerful and commanding.

The bear stopped eating, but did not look up. It must be a mistake. Whoever it was would soon go away and leave him in peace.

'Iorek Byrnison,' repeated the voice. 'My name is Farder Coram, of the Western Gyptians. May I speak to you?'

Annoyed but curious, Iorek decided to give the stranger his full attention. Angrily, he dropped the reindeer meat and reared up to his full height. On his hind legs, Iorek measured well over three metres. He towered above the man who'd dared to speak to him. Surprised, he noticed a smaller figure – a young girl. She took a step back. Like all humans, she had a dæmon. This was a special part of her soul that existed outside of her body in animal form. The girl's dæmon, which was in the shape of a cat, sat trembling on her shoulder.

'Well?' he roared.

'We want to offer you employment,' said Farder Coram. He did not seem at all afraid of the bear.

Iorek was not used to this. Whenever he spoke, people backed away and cowered in fear. They certainly didn't answer back. What was *wrong* with this man? 'I *am* employed,' he growled, 'by the townspeople. I mend broken machinery and articles of iron. I lift heavy objects.'

'What kind of work is that for a Panserbjørne?' asked Farder Coram, who was either very brave or very stupid.

The bear dropped to all fours, the ground trembling as his great weight made contact. It sounded as though the man wanted to hire him to fight. This was too much – it was bringing back painful memories of the life Iorek had once enjoyed. 'Paid work,' he growled in a voice that invited no argument.

At that moment, the back door of Einarsson's Bar creaked open and light spilled into the yard. A man crept outside, glancing around nervously before quickly setting down a brimming earthenware jar. He flinched as the huge bear turned to watch, and scurried back indoors as fast as he could. The door slammed shut.

Iorek strode towards the jar. With his back turned to Farder Coram and the girl, he lifted the jug high, pouring a stream of treacly brown liquid into his mouth. As he swallowed, a fiery heat flooded through him and he relaxed slightly.

'Is that what they pay you?' the girl asked.

The bear stopped drinking. How dare this child disturb him when he was enjoying the only pleasure left to him? He fastened his eyes on her, enjoying the feeling of power it gave him.

The girl and her dæmon shivered, as if with cold.

Abruptly, Iorek went on with his drinking. Soon, he would care about nothing – not this girl, not his sorry excuse for a life, nothing.

'Come, child,' said Farder Coram softly. 'The aeronaut was mistaken.'

He went to leave and the girl started after him, but suddenly she appeared to change her mind. She stopped and looked back.

'Iorek Byrnison!' she exclaimed, her voice rough with emotion. 'You're the first Ice Bear I ever met. I was ever so excited … and scared. But now I'm just disappointed. I heard that bears live to hunt and to fight. Why are you wasting your time here, letting the townspeople tell you what to do?'

There was a dreadful silence.

The mighty Iorek Byrnison stood motionless as the words sank in. Nobody spoke to him like this, least of all a child, and anger rumbled deep within him. He dropped the earthenware jar to the ground, where it smashed into many jagged pieces. The precious liquid seeped away.

A horrified Farder Coram tried to drag the girl away, but even if they had fled, Iorek would have been too fast for them. As swift as lightning, the bear moved forward.

Even though the child's dæmon crept inside her coat, she herself showed no fear. Instead, she boldly stared back at Iorek, waiting for his reply.

'I stay because the men of this town let me drink till I was asleep, and they took my armour away, and without that I cannot go to war,' he explained bitterly. 'And I am an armoured bear; war is the sea I swim in and the air I breathe. Without my armour...' He paused, hardly able to utter the words. 'I am nothing.'

The girl looked sympathetic. 'But ... can't you make more?' she asked. 'I thought bears were good at that, ironworking and such. And there's all this metal around.' She pointed vaguely to the untidy piles of junk that surrounded them, glinting in the last of the day's light.

Iorek sighed. This child obviously required more than explanations before she would leave him alone. He would give her proof. Wordlessly, he picked up a thick piece of metal and flourished a claw. Then, with no more effort than it took to tear paper, he casually ripped a great gash in the metal.

'Worthless,' said the bear. 'My armour is made for me of sky-iron – from the falling stars that land in Svalbard.' He thought wistfully of the flaming rocks that crashed to earth – so much more wonderful than scrap metal – then took a deep breath and continued. 'A bear's armour is his soul, as your dæmon is *your* soul,' he said. 'Irreplacable. You may as well take *him* away and replace him with a doll.'

Tears glistened in the girl's eyes. 'I couldn't live without Pan,' she whispered, clearly understanding Iorek's predicament at last. Her beloved dæmon Pantalaimon – Pan for short – meant everything to Lyra. It was inconceivable to be without him. 'That'd be worse than being dead. It must've been terrible, to lose your armour.'

'It was no less than I deserved,' muttered the bear, feeling hot with shame. He saw her curious stare and hung his head. 'I am an exile,' he said. 'I was sent away from Svalbard because I was unworthy. I fought another bear in single combat and was defeated.' Unable to stand the girl's pity for a second longer, he turned and trudged back towards the junkyard.

'Come, child,' said the man softly.

'But Farder Coram—' she began.

'We can't involve ourselves, Lyra,' he interrupted. 'It's too risky.'

Slowly, they walked away.

CHAPTER TWO

*J*orek Byrnison heard their footsteps clink across the ice. It was a sad sound. Forlornly, he returned to his work and chose a damaged motor-sledge from the heap of junk. His own problems might be impossible to solve, but at least he could fix this hunk of twisted metal. He lifted the vehicle casually and turned it back and forth, bending the whole heavy sheet back into shape. As he worked, the dents sprang out and it began to look like the sleek sledge it had once been. Deftly, he flipped the massive motor-sledge on its side and examined the runner.

He was so intent on his work that he didn't realize that the girl had stopped in her tracks. He didn't see her fiddling with a shiny, golden object that resembled a compass. And even if he had, he wouldn't have realized what it was, for this 'compass' was in fact an alethiometer

– a special device that could provide truthful answers to questions that Lyra formed in her mind. After the young girl had finished her questioning, she sprinted back in Iorek's direction, her step so light that the bear didn't even notice her as she approached him.

'Iorek Byrnison?'

The bear looked round. Although he was astonished to see the young girl and her dæmon again, he hid his emotions behind a steely gaze. Farder Coram was nowhere to be seen.

The girl took a step towards the bear.

'Don't,' her dæmon warned, as if determined that they should keep their distance from the fearsome creature. Pantalaimon stood at the girl's feet, his fur bristling.

'*I* won't,' he said, refusing to move.

Without breaking eye contact with the little cat-dæmon, the girl took another step in Iorek's direction. The Ice Bear watched them with interest.

'Lyra!' Pantalaimon cried desperately. 'Farder Coram said *no!*'

She took another step.

Stubbornly, the little cat dug his claws into

the icy ground. 'Stop!' he yelped. 'It hurts!'

The girl kept on walking – drawing closer to the bear and moving further and further from her dæmon. Iorek could see that this hurt her as much as it hurt her dæmon. Her face was screwed up with pain and each step away from the cat just made it worse. The bond of energy that connected her to her dæmon enabled them to share each other's thoughts, feelings and sensations, but it was like an invisible strand of elastic – and the more it stretched, the more it hurt them both.

By now, the dæmon was writhing in agony, bracing himself against the unbearable pull of his human. The girl cast a glance over her shoulder before looking back at the mighty Ice Bear. Slowly, painfully, she made her way towards Iorek Byrnison with grim determination, only stopping when they were eye to eye. The little cat-dæmon was so far away now that the girl could barely hold herself on the spot.

'Lyra!' groaned Pantalaimon. With a sob, he flew towards her, unable to stay apart a second longer. He flew into his human's arms and clung to her unhappily. Both of them seemed very shaken.

'Well?' asked Iorek curiously. The girl had his attention now. If what she had to say was so important that she would almost tear herself

away from the creature that was part of her very soul, then it was worth hearing.

But before Lyra could reply, the worried voice of Farder Coram suddenly rang out behind her. 'Lyra! Come back! It's not safe!' He sounded very scared, as if he feared Iorek might threaten to harm the young girl at any moment.

Ignoring the Gyptian, Lyra stood her ground and addressed Iorek directly.

'I know where your armour is,' she began. 'They tricked you out of it. They shouldn't have done that, Iorek Byrnison. It's in the district office of the Magisterium.' She paused, perhaps searching for the right words. 'They think it's got an evil spirit in it … and they want to exorcise it.'

Iorek heard the words, but they didn't sink in. 'I must work till sunset,' he said stubbornly. The last of the sun cast a slight warmth over his face – until it set, he was unable to concentrate on anything but the task in hand. 'I gave my word. I still owe a few minutes' work.' He stared into the distance, where a sliver of orange light glowed above the horizon.

Lyra looked up at him, a small figure dwarfed by his great height. 'The sun's set where I am,' she said brightly.

Iorek dropped to all fours and saw that nearer the ground it was indeed dark. 'That is true,' he said. And suddenly, his tired mind began to whirr with new thoughts. He realized that he'd been a fool. All this time, he'd toiled away mending scrap metal, while his beloved armour had been so near! He looked closely at the girl who'd brought him such unbelievable news. She stared back at him, her eyes honest and true. 'What is your name, child?' he said slowly.

'Lyra Belacqua,' she replied solemnly.

Iorek's mind was made up at once. 'Then I owe you a debt, Lyra Belacqua,' he said. 'I will serve you in your campaign until I am dead … or you have a victory.' And, without another word, he turned on his heel and charged away.

He had waited long enough.

It was time for action.

CHAPTER THREE

*I*orek Byrnison galloped through narrow streets towards the centre of Trollesund. With his teeth bared in anger, he was a truly terrifying sight. The frozen ground shook under the weight of his pounding paws as he hurtled closer to his beloved armour.

Vaguely, Iorek heard the townspeople scream as he tore past, but he didn't even break his stride. He was heading for the Magisterial Residence and nothing and no one would stop him.

He soon reached the town square. There it was – the old brick building that held his armour. With a deft flick of his mighty paw, the oak doors were splintered beyond repair … and the mighty Ice Bear was inside. Workers scuttled away from him, shrieking and wailing in terror.

Iorek headed down the main corridor, his keen eyes scanning the rooms he passed for any glimpse of sky iron. Nothing. He carried on searching, batting aside anyone foolish enough to stand in his path.

And then … he found it.

Iorek's eyes lit up with pleasure as he peered into a darkened cell and saw the heap of rusting metal. His long-lost armour was locked in the Magisterial vaults. At once, he grasped the thick iron bars that held it prisoner. The bars were no match for Iorek's awesome strength, and he bent them effortlessly with his huge paws. The bear touched the discoloured metal of his armour tenderly. It looked old and uncared for, but he knew that he could fix it – just like the motor-sledge.

Bang! Bang! Bang!

The guards were firing at him. Iorek felt tiny pricks of pain and quickly slid the interlocking sheets of metal over his head. The guard's bullets pinged harmlessly off the sky-iron shielding. Now he was safely clad in his trusty armour, Iorek Byrnison felt stronger and more powerful than he had in a very long time. He was ready for anything.

Looking up, he saw that Magisterial guards were closing in. It was time to leave.

Iorek decided that it would be foolish to retrace his steps through the building – by now, it was sure to be swarming with his enemies. Instead, he would take a short cut. The bear ducked into a small office and, with a great roar, burst through the outer wall. Bricks exploded outwards as he emerged from the Magisterial district office into the town square.

There was a huge gasp of astonishment from the gathered crowd as the Ice Bear reared up on his hind legs, towering high above everyone. He was an impressive sight. The metal of his precious armour was rust-red and crudely riveted together. Great sheets and plates of dented, tarnished metal scraped and screeched as they moved against each other. Everyone agreed – Iorek Byrnison of the Panserbjørne was terrifying.

The bear took one look at the waiting police and prepared to charge. The police raised their weapons, ready to fire a volley of gunshots, but he was not afraid. Iorek filled his lungs with icy-cold fresh air and—

'Iorek!' cried a small voice from somewhere beneath his elbow. Lyra grabbed a handful of the dirty, matted fur between the plates of armour. 'Iorek Byrnison!' she pleaded. 'Please don't fight! What they done en't right, I know ... but if you fight, you'll kill them and there'll be more fighting and we'll never get away!'

The great Ice Bear was stunned at the girl's bravery. And, realising that she spoke the truth, he nodded and relaxed his tensed muscles a little. Perhaps killing was not the answer

– at least, not today.

'Now's your chance!' shouted the Magisterial Commissar eagerly. 'Ready to fire! Aim!' As the police clicked shut the bolts of their rifles, the Commissar opened his mouth ready to give the command ... and came face to face with the long barrel of a revolver.

'Let's not be too hasty,' said a tall, thin man with startlingly blue eyes. His mouth was twisted into a wry smile. 'Way I see it, there's no need for a dust-up.'

Iorek recognized the man immediately. This was Lee Scoresby – aeronaut for hire. They knew each other well.

'Howdy, Iorek,' said the man, turning towards the bear. 'I was down south, heard you ran into a little local trouble. Didn't have the first notion of how to spring you.' He nodded at Lyra. 'Fortunately, little girls come real resourceful down in these parts.'

Iorek Byrnison grunted in agreement. Then he looked back at the guns, which were still pointing at him. But more people had now begun to arrive. Gyptians – water travellers that roamed canals and rivers – clustered around Scoresby. Among them was John Faa, who Iorek knew to be their leader. So these people were on Scoresby's side too... And now that the situation was no longer so one-sided, the police were looking increasingly unsure of success.

'Lookee here,' the aeronaut drawled, glancing around at the Gyptians before directing his steely gaze back at the Commissar. 'Reinforcements. What do you say you fellas just call it a day?' He lowered his pistol.

The Magisterial Commissar, who seemed thoroughly disappointed that there had been no bloodshed, angrily gathered up what remained of his shattered dignity – and retreated.

Most of the townspeople followed his lead and started to make their way home too. The entertainment was over for the day.

Lee Scoresby turned to Iorek with a friendly grin. 'I've just been hired on by these gentlemen of the Gyptian persuasion,' he said. 'You figurin' to join this turkey shoot?'

Iorek Byrnison didn't hesitate for a second. After all, there was only one answer to give. 'Yes,' he said firmly, remembering his promise. 'I have a contract with the child.'

Lyra smiled happily at him, and Iorek knew he'd made the right choice.

CHAPTER FOUR

*T*he Gyptian war party was leaving town. Dressed in their very warmest clothes and furs, they snaked across the icy wasteland, dragging a line of heavily laden baggage sledges after them.

Lee Scoresby watched nervously as large pieces of his huge airship were hauled on to the few remaining sledges. 'Careful now, fellas,' he said, through gritted teeth. 'Airship machinery's kind of finicky. I want to die in a rocking chair, not a hydrogen fire.'

Iorek Byrnison was among the last to leave. Now he knew the full story behind Lyra's campaign, he was even more determined to help. The young girl and her Gyptian allies were heading for Bolvangar, in search of the Gyptian children who'd been stolen by the Gobblers – the name people had given to the sinister individuals behind the kidnappings.

Lyra – quite obviously the most important person here – was also looking for her missing friend Roger; she suspected that he too had been snatched and taken to Bolvangar. No one knew how or why the children had been abducted, but they were going to find out – and Iorek was going to do everything in his power to help them.

After just hours of freedom, no one would have recognized this mighty bear as being the bedraggled, miserable creature from the junkyard. His clean fur was pure white and his eyes sparkled with excitement. But the biggest difference was his armour. Iorek had quickly dispatched a plump seal – it had been an excellent meal – and then spent hours rubbing slippery seal blubber all over the discoloured metal. Every plate, every crevice, every joint had been oiled until it was as good as new. Now, when he moved, there was not the slightest squeak.

Iorek watched Lyra march past, her expression serious and determined. Lost in her own thoughts, the young girl did not see the Gyptian in her path struggling with a particularly large and cumbersome section of Lee Scoresby's airship and he bumped into her, dislodging a tin mug and stoppered jar from her bag. The objects fell to the ground, a curious fluttering, knocking sound coming from within the jar.

Lyra rushed to pick up the object, but Iorek was there first. He retreived the glass jar from where it had fallen and regarded it with interest. Inside, a curious, metallic insect buzzed angrily at him. Quickly, the bear squeezed the stopper home before it could escape. From Lyra's expression, it was very clear that she wanted whatever was in the jar to stay there. But the glass jar was so fragile – if the strange creature were to remain imprisoned, its jail needed to be more secure.

Iorek took the mug and speedily cut a band of tin from its rim using his claw. Next, he deftly flattened the rest of the mug and scored out two metal circles. Popping open the jar's stopper, he trapped the insect between his claws and then, with incredible speed, he sandwiched the creature between the two circles. Finally, he wrapped the band of metal around the circles' edges and pressed them into place. A furious, but muffled buzzing could be heard from inside. But there was no question of escape now.

Flashing the bear a look of gratitude, Lyra took the tin and returned it to her bag. Together, they joined the Gyptians on their long walk across the ice and Lyra began to explain about the strange insect. It was a spy-fly – a clockwork creature running on evil energy. It had been sent to attack her, but the Gyptians had captured it instead and now it was trapped. Thanks to Iorek, the spy-fly now remained trapped.

***

Soon, they'd left Trollesund far behind and were travelling through a forested valley and out into a snowy world. Lyra had been talking for quite some time and showed no sign of slowing, but Iorek found himself fascinated by her lively speech. He'd never met anyone quite like Lyra before. She was kind and charming when she wanted to be, but feisty and quick to anger too. In fact, Iorek now knew virtually all there was to know about Lyra – from the fact she hated lessons to the adventures she'd shared with her dæmon, Pantalaimon. 'But I don't like people telling me what to do,' she continued. 'I bet you don't like it either. I can tell.'

The bear nodded in agreement.

Lyra put her head on one side. 'You're like my Uncle Asriel,' she said thoughtfully. 'He's all rough and noble like you, that's what I think...'

They walked on, following the Gyptians up the slope of a glacier and making for the pass between the two sides of the fjord. The Gyptians' boots sank in the snow as they tried to keep the sledges upright and they left deep footprints behind them.

Iorek Byrnison felt a shiver of excitement as he looked at the bleak, forbidding landscape stretching in every direcction. It was very cold and getting colder.

It was like coming home.

That night, they made camp beneath the brilliant glow of a million twinkling stars. The only sound was the mournful tune of Lee Scoresby's harmonica. At the edge of the camp, Iorek sat motionless on his haunches, his back to the warmth of the roaring fire.

'Ior—' began Lyra.

'What is it, child?' he replied wearily.

'Oh,' she said. 'I thought you were asleep.'

Iorek turned to look at her, the small girl with the power to drag him across continents. He wondered what more she could have to say – she'd spoken almost non-stop all day.

'Is it hard not having a dæmon?' she said gently. 'Don't you get lonely?'

'Lonely?' said Iorek. It was a difficult question. 'I don't know. They tell me the ice is cold – I don't know what cold is, because I don't freeze. So I don't know what lonely means either. Bears are meant to be solitary.' He paused and looked up. He sensed that there was more to come. 'But that is not what you have come to ask me.'

'No…' Lyra frowned and she paused before speaking. 'Iorek, the alethiometer keeps telling me something. In the next valley there's a lake with a house by it, and it's troubled by a ghost. It's something to do with the Gobblers – and Roger…' She faltered briefly at the mention of her best

friend's name. Earlier, she'd told Iorek how Roger had vanished. She'd also told how she'd once made Roger a promise – that if anything were ever to happen to her friend, she would rescue him. She meant to honour this promise. Lyra had looked deadly serious when she said this to the great bear.

'You could take me there, couldn't you?' she continued now. 'The Gyptians... Well, they wouldn't let me. They'd want to protect me. But *you* could carry me there and back before

anyone knows, couldn't you?' Her eyes pleaded with him.

Iorek wasn't sure he'd heard right. 'You wish ... to *ride* on me?' he asked.

'Yes,' said Lyra.

The bear thought quickly, before shrugging off the plates of sky iron. 'We will travel faster without armour,' he said.

CHAPTER FIVE

I orek burst over the top of the ridge in a shower of icy particles that glittered and twinkled in the bright moonlight. He galloped across the snowy plateau. For the first time in a very long time he felt truly alive – as if he could do *anything*. He was Iorek Byrnison of the Panserbjørne once again, a mighty force to be reckoned with. He almost forgot about the small girl clinging to his fur; to Iorek, Lyra weighed no more than a feather.

Onwards they went, making their way carefully around a mountain peak and then slip-sliding down, down, down the other side. They soon reached a lake nestling in the bottom of a deep valley. At its edge, the water was frozen into shards of ice that sparkled like quartz crystals, tinkling and chiming as the wind blew them against each other. It was a beautiful, but eerie sound.

Suddenly, Iorek felt a prickling sensation – as if they were not alone. He looked up and saw a crowd of black shapes streaming northwards through the night sky.

'Are those birds?' asked Lyra, wide-eyed with wonderment.

'Witches…' muttered Iorek. This wasn't good. 'More than I have ever seen before.'

'What are they doing?' said his small, inquisitive passenger.

'Flying to war, maybe,' Iorek replied. 'This is a sight to frighten Lord Faa. If they are flying to the aid of your enemies, you should all be afraid.'

'Are *you* afraid?' Lyra asked.

'Not yet,' Iorek said honestly. 'When I am, I will master my fear.' He spotted twinkling lights in the distance and slowed to a walk.

'We are near,' he said.

Lyra slid to the ground and continued the journey at Iorek's side. After a few steps, she placed a small hand on the bear's fur, as if seeking to gain courage from him.

Together, they reached the frozen lake and saw an abandoned trapper's hut at the edge of the ice. The wind sang through the loose planking, producing a loud moaning noise.

The hut was dark, ugly and evil-looking, with a bear's head nailed up at the door. It made Iorek angry to see such a fine creature displayed in this way. 'This is a Samoyed hut,' he said. 'Hunters and marauders. No one is here now, but there is something...'

'What?' asked Lyra.

'Not natural,' finished Iorek. He stepped forward, lifting a paw to push open the door. 'I will make sure the way is safe,' he said.

Lyra stopped him. 'No,' she whispered. 'I had better go in alone. You might frighten whatever's inside.'

Iorek couldn't help noticing that she was trembling, as if she was very frightened herself. He felt a sudden rush of admiration for the girl. There were few people in the world this brave. Slowly, he nodded to Lyra. He would stand guard outside to make sure no harm came to her.

'No! Don't go in!' cried Pantalaimon. The dæmon ran back and forth in front of Lyra, uttering strange little frightened sounds. 'Bad ... something bad! Don't go in!' he squeaked in fear.

Lyra took a deep breath. 'Pan, for God's sake,' she pleaded. 'Help me.'

Looking very unhappy, the little cat-dæmon scuttled quickly to her side, where he crouched in terror.

Iorek watched as Lyra went up to the hut, which was blackened with smoke. Slowly, she released the door's reindeer-skin latch and pushed it open. 'Hello?' she said cautiously. 'Come out. Come out!'

There was no response, just the eerie wail of the wind.

Pantalaimon was terrified. 'Go away!' the little dæmon begged, hurling himself into Lyra's arms. 'Don't stay there! Oh, Lyra … go now! Turn back!'

'Hush, Pan,' whispered Lyra. 'We've got to master our fear.' She took a cautious step forward, holding her dæmon still against her. 'Hello... Hello...' she said softly.

Lyra and Pantalaimon disappeared inside the trapper's hut.

Iorek stared after them, feelings of pride and fear doing battle inside him. If anything happened to the girl, he would never forgive himself. He crept closer to the window, but he could hear nothing but the low sound of Lyra's voice. Occasionally, the murmuring rose higher – but whether it was with surprise or fright, the Ice Bear couldn't tell. With difficulty, he remained where he was.

It seemed hours – but was probably minutes – later that Lyra and Pantalaimon emerged slowly from the hut.

Iorek saw with shock that the girl and her dæmon were not alone.

A little boy clung desperately to Lyra's hand, huddling close to her. He was shivering and filthy and looked utterly lost. But there was something much more terrible to see.

This child had no dæmon.

CHAPTER SIX

As Iorek padded through the snow back towards the Gyptian campsite, he felt a cold chill settle in his heart. And it was nothing to do with the cold. It was all to do with the poor boy that Lyra had found. *All* humans had dæmons, he thought, so why not this child? Without a dæmon, a human was just half a person – Iorek wasn't even sure they could survive.

On the way, Lyra explained to Iorek that she knew the boy. He was Billy Costa, a Gyptian and one of the many children who had been kidnapped by the Gobblers. These were the very children they were searching for.

At last, they reached the Gyptian campsite. A large group of people came out to meet them, with John Faa and Farder Coram leading the way. But the crowd slowed when they spotted the mutilated boy and formed a semi-circle around Iorek and his passengers. Only John Faa, the Gyptian leader, had the courage to step forward and help Lyra down from Iorek's back.

'Gracious God,' breathed Farder Coram. 'What is this? Lyra, child, what have you found?'

Lyra and Pan slid to the ground, closely followed by the boy. 'It's Billy,' said Lyra. 'Billy Costa.' She lowered her voice. 'They took away his dæmon.'

A wave of horror and anger rushed through the crowd, but still the Gyptians hung back.

Then one woman burst through the ranks. 'Billy?' said Ma Costa.

Billy Costa stood before her, swaying unsteadily. Despite his rescue, he still looked lost, still miserable. And he showed no sign of recognizing his own mother.

But Ma Costa knew him at once. She ran to the boy, wrapping her arms around him and holding him close as she cried bitterly. 'Thank you, Lyra,' she said between sobs. 'Thank you!'

Billy stared unseeingly at the assembled people. 'They took Ratter away…' he murmured to himself. 'Why did they do that? It hurts…'

'Hush, Billy,' said Ma Costa. 'We'll find your dæmon. We'll bring her back.'

Billy looked at his mother and frowned. 'Who are you?' he asked curiously.

The crowd gasped in horror.

'Don't you know me, Billy?' Ma Costa said to her troubled son.

Billy was silent for a moment. 'Where's Ratter?' he said.

Suddenly, there was a whistling noise, closely followed by furious shouting and the crack of gunfire. Iorek steadied himself for battle – the Gyptian camp was under attack.

Arrows rained down on the camp and

the Gyptians quickly prepared to defend themselves. They fired into the darkness around the campfires, but the flickering flames had blinded them. The enemy had the advantage.

John Faa fired his pistol at a shadowy form moving at the edge of the camp and it dropped to the ground. But a moment later, the Gyptian leader was hit by an arrow and he too fell.

Meanwhile, Iorek was doing his best to keep the invisible enemy at bay. With one swipe, he knocked an attacker off his feet, then cast his eye about for the girl. Where *was* she? Then, his eyes locked on to her. As if in slow motion, dark figures surrounded Lyra, lifting her from her feet, stifling her cries. They tied her hands and yanked a hood over her head.

As he started towards them, the armoured bear heard a faint cry. 'Iorek! Iorek Byrnison! Help me!' Then the struggling girl was bundled out of sight.

Iorek thundered across the camp, with little thought for anything in his path. But by the time he reached the spot where he'd last seen her, Lyra was gone.

Desperately, Iorek stared into the darkness of the icy wasteland. But he could see nothing. And the only sound was that of a sledge hissing across the snow, the noise rapidly disappearing into the distance.

The bear threw back his head and roared with anger. He was furious – with the kidnappers who had taken his Lyra away and with himself for letting them do it. But they wouldn't get away with it. Iorek Byrnison would find her, this small girl who had so impressed him with her courage and determination. He roared in fury once more – he had a contract with the child, and he would rescue Lyra, even if was the last thing he ever did.

GLOSSARY

The world of the Golden Compass is a world very much like ours, in a parallel universe. Much of it would be familiar to us – the continents, the oceans, Brytain, Norroway and the North Pole … but much is shockingly different. On this parallel Earth, a person's soul lives on the outside of their body, in the form of a dæmon – a talking animal spirit that accompanies them through life. A child's dæmon can change shape, assuming all the forms that a child's infinite potential inspires; but as a person ages, their dæmon gradually settles into one form, according to their character and nature.

CHARACTERS

Lyra

Lyra Belacqua is a twelve-year-old girl who has been left by her Uncle Asriel to be raised by the scholars and fellows of Jordan College in Oxford, Brytain. Headstrong, rebellious and wilful, Lyra's carefree existence comes to an end after numerous children, including her friend Roger, mysteriously begin to disappear. Lyra's dæmon is Pantalaimon (Pan).

Farder Coram

One of the leaders of the Western Gyptians who becomes a friend to Lyra. Farder Coram brings Lyra closer to fulfilling her destiny by working with her on deciphering the multi-layered meanings conveyed by the Golden Compass.

Gyptians

A nomadic group of waterfarers who live on canal-boats, the Gyptians are the descendants of warriors and traders from the east. Lyra falls under the protection of the Western Gyptians led by John Faa and his chief adviser, Farder Coram. Together they voyage North to rescue the children – of every origin – abducted by the Gobblers.

The Gobblers

A sinister band of kidnappers who abduct the children of the poor and the marginalized – orphans, servant children, Gyptians – and take them North for unknown purposes.

Iorek Byrnison

Iorek Byrnison is an Ice Bear, or as they are known and feared throughout Lyra's world, a Panserbjørne. A warrior-for-hire like the rest of his folk, Iorek has fallen on hard times. His armour – which to a bear represents his very soul – has been stolen. When Lyra helps Iorek get his armour back, she earns the eternal gratitude and loyalty of the fierce bear.

Lee Scoresby

Honest, loyal, with a great sense of duty and honour, Lee is an aeronaut from the country of Texas. With an airship at his command, he is hired by the Gyptians to help Lyra find her friend Roger as well as the Gyptians' missing children. His dæmon is a hare named Hester.

❧———————— DEFINITIONS ————————❧

Alethiometer

Also known as the Golden Compass, the alethiometer is an extraordinarily intricate device that was made in the sixteenth century. Its needle seeks out, instead of true North, Truth itself. Reading the alethiometer is a difficult task, but Lyra Belacqua possesses a natural ability to use the instrument.

The Magisterium

The powerful organization that dominates the politics and society of Lyra's world, in Brytain and beyond. It has established a ruthless, iron-grip on the nations of the world.

There are worlds beyond our own
— the Compass will show the way …

THE GOLDEN COMPASS™

Read all three books and follow the exciting
adventures of Pan, Iorek and the Golden Monkey!

 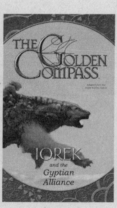 

Pan and the
Prisoners of Bolvangar

Iorek and the
Gyptian Alliance

The Golden Monkey and the
Duel of the Dæmons